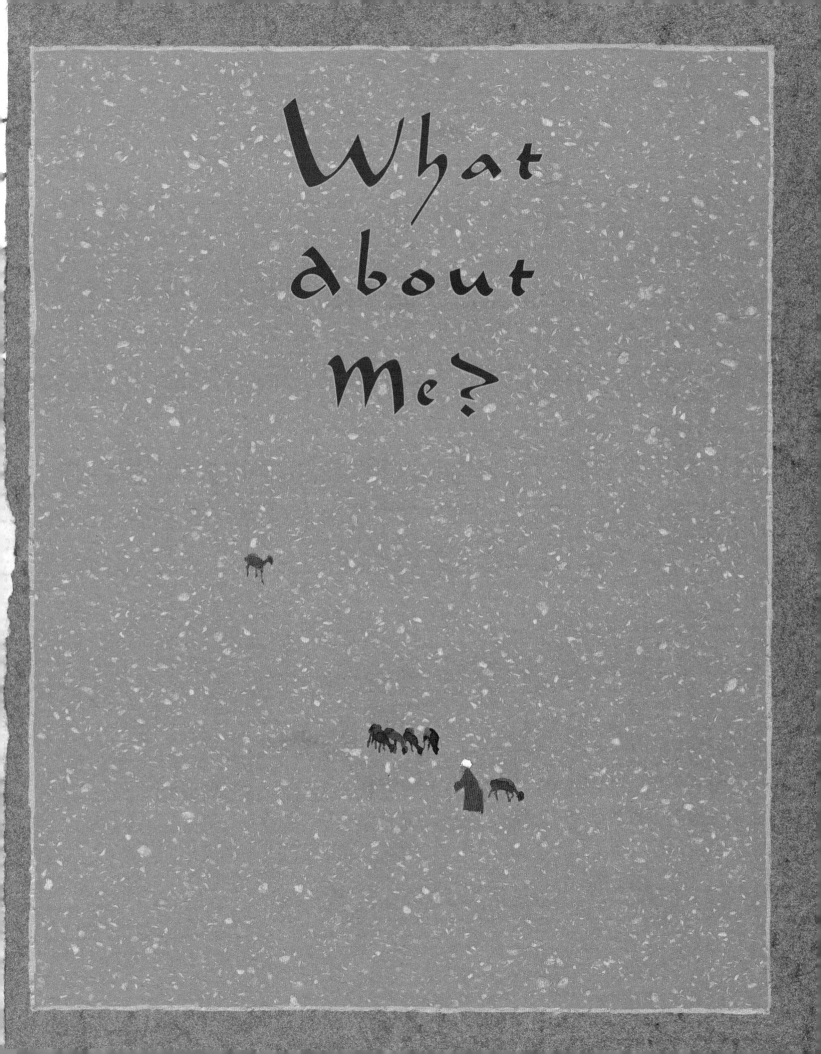

As all good tales have their sources, this one is rooted in the Sufi tradition. The Sufi, wise masters and disciples of a religion whose origin is in the Middle East, have passed down these tales for thousands of years. Sufi teaching-tales, like the tales of Aesop, are fables that entertain as they teach. Their clever construction and witty conclusions bring pleasure to young and old, while their morals provide subtle wisdom and truth for all.

PATRICIA LEE GAUCH, EDITOR

PHILOMEL BOOKS,
a division of Penguin Putnam Books for Young Readers,
345 Hudson Street, New York, NY 10014.
Philomel Books, Reg. U.S. Pat. & Tm. Off. Published simultaneously in Canada.
Printed in Hong Kong by South China Printing Co. (1988) Ltd.

Book design by Semadar Megged.   The text is set in 19-point Calligraph 421 BT.
The illustrations are rendered in collage and watercolor.

Library of Congress Cataloging-in-Publication Data
Young, Ed. What about me? / Ed Young. p. cm.
Summary: A young boy determinedly follows the instructions of the Grand Master in the hope of
gaining knowledge, only to be surprised as how he acquires it. Based on a Sufi tale.
[1. Sufis—Folklore. 2. Folklore—Middle East.] I. Title. PZ8.1.Y84 Bo 2002 398.2'088'297—dc21
[E] 2001045927 ISBN 0-399-23624-4
1 3 5 7 9 10 8 6 4 2
First Impression

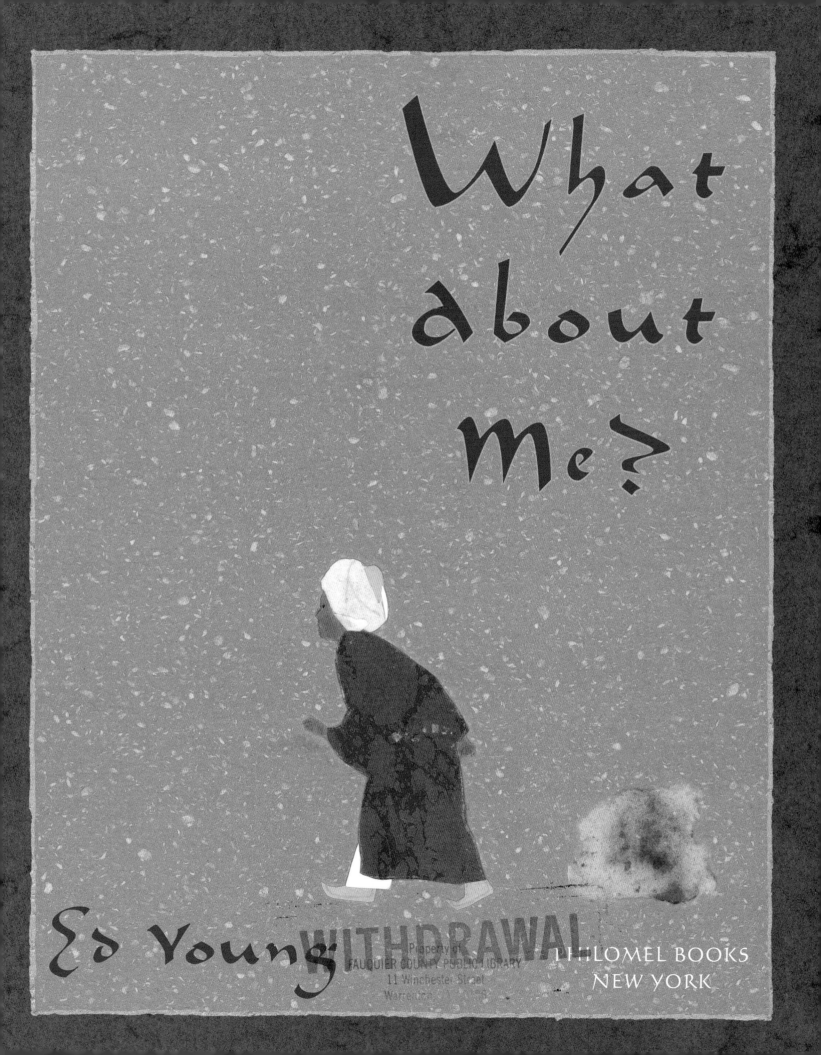

What about Me?

Ed Young

PHILOMEL BOOKS
NEW YORK

ONCE THERE WAS A BOY who wanted knowledge, but he did not know how to gain it. "I shall see a Grand Master," he said. "He has plenty. Perhaps he will give me some." When he arrived, he bowed and said, "Grand Master, you are wise. How may I gain a little bit of your knowledge?"

The Grand Master said, "You need to bring me a small carpet for my work." The boy hurried off to find a carpetmaker.

"Carpetmaker," he said, "I need a small carpet to give to the Grand Master for his work."

The carpetmaker barked, "He has needs! What about me? I need thread for weaving my carpets. Bring me some thread and I will make you a carpet."

So the boy went off to find a spinner woman.

He found her at last. "Spinner Woman," he said, "I need some thread for the carpetmaker, who will make me a carpet to give to the Grand Master for his work."

"You need thread!" she wheezed. "What about me? I need goat hair to make the thread. Get me some and you can have your thread."

So the boy went off looking for someone who kept goats.

When he came to a goatkeeper, the boy told him his needs. "Your needs! The others' needs! What about me? You need goat hair to buy knowledge—I need goats to provide the hair! Get me some goats and I will help you."

The boy ran off again to find someone who sold goats. When he found
such a man, the boy told him of his
problems, and the goatseller said,
"What do I know about thread or carpets, or Grand Masters? I need a pen
to keep my goats in—they are straying
all over the place! Get me a pen, and
you can have a goat or two."

The boy's head buzzed. "Everyone has a need," he mumbled to himself as he hurried off. "And what of my need for knowledge?" But he went to a carpenter who made pens, and he gave the carpenter his long story.

"Say no more," the carpenter said. "Yes, I make pens, but I need a wife and no one will have me. Find me a wife and we can talk about your problems."

So the boy went off, going from house to house.

Finally he met a matchmaker. "Yes, I know such a girl—she will make a good wife, but I have a need. All my life, I have wanted . . ."

"Yes?" said the boy.

"Knowledge," said the matchmaker. "Bring me knowledge, and I will give you the young girl's name to take to the carpenter."

The boy was stunned. "But . . . but we cannot get knowledge without a carpet, no carpet without thread, no thread without hair, no hair without a goat, no goat without a pen, no pen without a wife for the carpenter."

"Stop!" said the matchmaker. "I for one don't want knowledge that bad." And she sent the boy away.

"I need a carpet," the boy chanted. "I need a carpet, I NEED A CARPET!"

And so he began to wander farther
and farther from his village.

Until one day he came to a village where he saw a merchant in the market-place, wringing his hands.

"Merchant," the young man said, "why do you wring your hands?"

The merchant looked at the young man's gentle face. "I have an only and beautiful daughter who I think is mad. I need help, but I don't know where to find it."

"I could not even get a piece of thread when I wanted it," said the young man. "But perhaps I can help."

And so the merchant led him to the girl. When she saw his kind face, she stopped ranting. "Oh, good young man," she said, "I have a need. My father wishes me to marry a merchant like himself, but I love a simple carpenter."

When she described the carpenter, the wanderer suddenly said, "Why, she loves the very carpenter I know!" And so he went to the other village, and took the girl and her secret to him.

In thanks, the carpenter immediately gave the young man wood for a pen.

The goatseller placed the goats in
the pen and gave him some goats,

which he took to the goatkeeper, who gave him some of their hair,

which he took to the spinner, who spun
him thread.

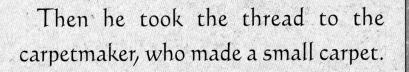

Then he took the thread to the
carpetmaker, who made a small carpet.

This small carpet he carried back to the Grand Master. When he arrived at the house of the wise man, he gave the carpet to him.

"And now, Grand Master, may I have knowledge?"

"But don't you know?" said the Grand Master.

The Grand Master's Morals are Two:

*S*ome of the most precious gifts that we receive
are those we receive when we are giving.

and

*O*ften, knowledge comes to us when we least expect it.